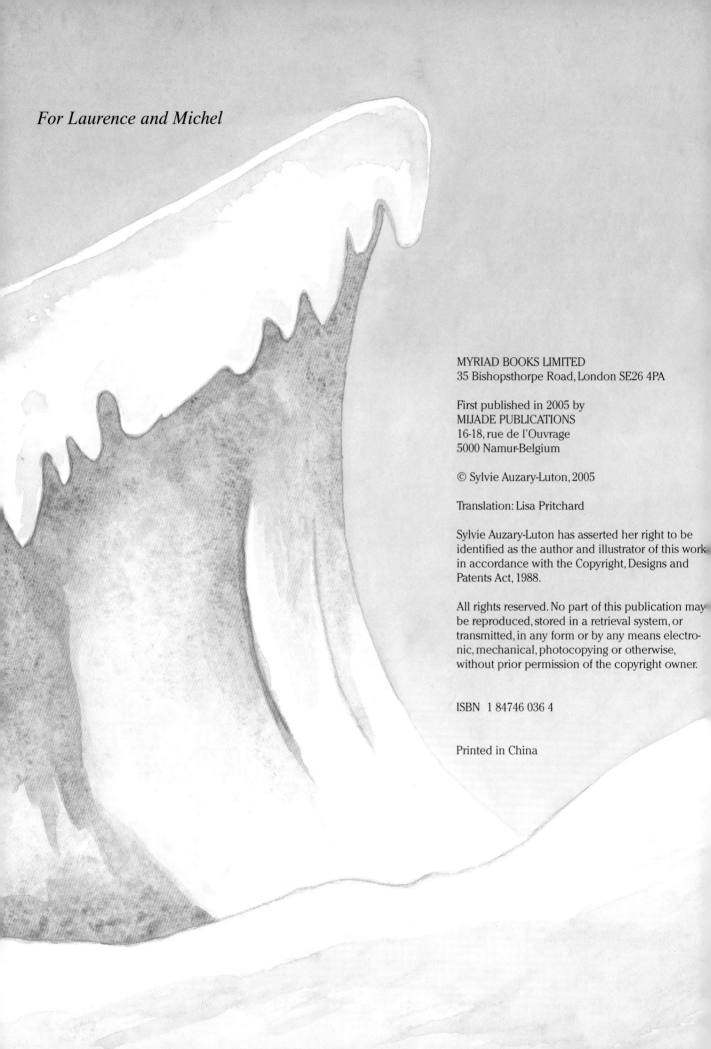

For Laurence and Michel

MYRIAD BOOKS LIMITED
35 Bishopsthorpe Road, London SE26 4PA

First published in 2005 by
MIJADE PUBLICATIONS
16-18, rue de l'Ouvrage
5000 Namur-Belgium

© Sylvie Auzary-Luton, 2005

Translation: Lisa Pritchard

ISBN 1 84746 036 4

Printed in China

Sylvie Auzary-Luton

Little Penguin's Stories

MYRIAD BOOKS LIMITED

Out on the ice, Little Penguin was feeling naughty.

"HELP!" he shouted. "There's a bear!"

The other penguins raced to his rescue. Where was the bear?

"Phew, it's gone," grinned Little Penguin.

Grandpa was very cross.

"Be careful, Little Penguin. If you tell lies, nobody will ever believe you."

Little Penguin decided to put on the skates that Sisi had lent him. He set off over the ice, jumping and twirling. BUMP! He crashed into a rock.

'Oh no, Sisi's skates are ruined!" Little Penguin took them off.
When Sisi saw them she said: "What happened to my skates?"
Little Penguin said, "There was a huge bear. It was so big it
squashed them when it tried to put them on. And then it ran away."
Sisi was amazed.

Quickly, Little Penguin said: "Come on, Mum's
got a picnic ready."

Little Penguin could see that Mum had put his favourite fish out for everyone to eat. But Little Penguin didn't want to share it. So he pointed to an iceberg and shouted:
"There's a big bear! It's coming to get us!"

All the penguins ran away...

... except Little Penguin. He gobbled up the whole fish.

When Mum came back, Little Penguin said:
'The bear came and gobbled up the whole fish,
then he went away. He didn't see me because I was hiding."

Mum knew he was lying. After all, a bear would
have eaten the rest of the picnic too.
"No pudding for a week, Little Penguin.
Maybe then you'll learn not to tell lies."

When the other penguins teased Little Penguin, he told them:
"I've got a secret friend. His name is Jules. He's VERY big and
VERY strong. We fought that bear together. Look, last time we
even pulled out his whiskers."

Little Penguin gave each of the other penguins what he
had in his hands. "Now that big old bear won't bother
us again. A bear without whiskers isn't dangerous."

Mum came out holding her broom. It looked strange.

'What have you been up to now?" she said.
'I didn't do it," said Little Penguin.

But Mum could see what Little Penguin's friends were holding, and she was very cross.

The other penguins were furious. "We're not
your friends any more. We're tired of all your stories.
You always tell lies!"

They chased Little Penguin away and threw snowballs at him.
Little Penguin turned round and started throwing snowballs
back at the others.

Suddenly they all shouted, "Little Penguin come back.
There's a bear!"

When Little Penguin turned
round he saw that it was
true. There really was a
bear, and it was standing
right behind him

The bear grabbed Little Penguin.
"So YOU are Little Penguin," it shouted. "I hear that you've been telling lots of stories about me, and none of them were true. I think I'll take you home and eat you for my dinner."

Little Penguin was so scared he couldn't say a word.

When the bear got home, it put Little Penguin in a cage.
It went to find a padlock to put on the cage door.

Just then another bear came in. It was even bigger!

"Excuse me Mr Bear," Little Penguin said very politely. "There is a rather large bear right behind you."

"Ha, ha! You can't fool me," laughed the bear. "I know you're a great big liar. Now don't interrupt me, I'm going to make a special sauce to go with boiled penguin for supper."

The other bear said, "Good idea – while you make the sauce, I'll eat the liar."

"WHAT!" roared the first bear. "That penguin's mine! I'm going to eat it."

The bears started to growl and then they began to fight.

Luckily for Little Penguin, the cage was still open. He climbed out and ran for his life.

Little Penguin ran as fast as his little legs could carry him.
He didn't look back. In the distance he could see all the
other penguins running towards him.

All his friends and Grandpa and Mum were there.
"We're coming, Little Penguin, we're coming to rescue you."
Little Penguin was very glad when he reached his mum and she
gave him a big hug.

"Your friends came to tell us that the big bear had caught you. How did you escape?" asked Grandpa.

"There were two bears, Grandpa," said Little Penguin. "The second one was even bigger than the one that caught me."

"Little Penguin, will you never learn? Don't start telling lies again," said Mum crossly.

"I promise you it's the truth, Mum. Please believe me. I'm never going to tell lies again. It was a very silly thing to do."

"Very wise," said Grandpa.
"Let's all go home and you
can tell us all about your
big adventure."